To Barney, my little shrimp - MB

LITTLE TIGER PRESS
1 The Coda Centre, 189 Munster Road, London SW6 6AW
www.littletiger.co.uk

First published in Great Britain 2014

Text and illustrations copyright © Matt Buckingham 2014

Matt Buckingham has asserted his right to
be identified as the author and illustrator of this work
under the Copyright, Designs and Patents Act, 1988

A CIP catalogue record for this book is available
from the British Library

Printed in China • LTP/1400/0752/1013
2 4 6 8 10 9 7 5 3 1

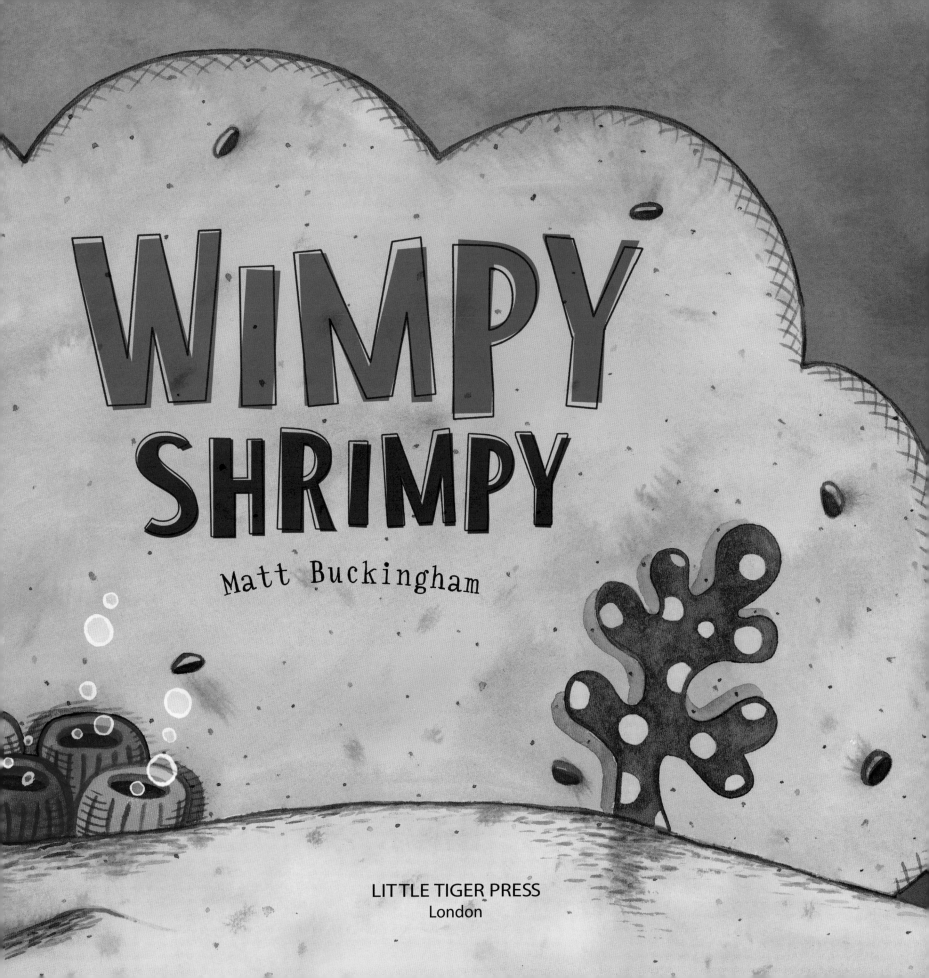

WIMPY
SHRIMPY

Matt Buckingham

LITTLE TIGER PRESS
London

Down at the bottom of the sea
lived a little shrimp. And this
little shrimp was a bit of a wimp.

When all his friends played happily,
Shrimpy was too scared to join in.

"Come and play hide-and-seek," called Turtle.
But Shrimpy wouldn't. He was too worried he'd get **LOST**.

"Oh, don't be **wimpy**, Shrimpy!" tutted Turtle.

"Play catch with us, Shrimpy," said Crab.

But Shrimpy thought the ball
might **SQUASH** him.
"Oh, don't be **wimpy,
Shrimpy!**" sighed Crab.

"What about hopscotch?" asked Octopus. "It's great!"
But Shrimpy was scared his legs would get **TANGLED IN A KNOT**.

"OH, **DON'T** BE **WIMPY,** SHRIMPY!" his friends all shouted.

"Please come and play," said Snail.
"You're missing all the fun. There's really
nothing to be afraid of."

But Shrimpy wouldn't play leapfrog, or follow-the-leader, or what time is it Mr Shark.

In fact, Shrimpy wouldn't do **ANYTHING**. He was too worried that something bad would happen.

What's the time, Mr Shark?

Oh dear!

Then one day something **DID** happen.
Nobody asked Shrimpy to play.

Suddenly Shrimpy felt very . . .

. . . lonely.

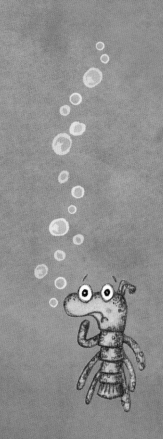

Shrimpy looked at his friends all playing.
Then he began to think. Nobody was
getting lost, or squashed, or in a tangle.

Everyone was just having **FUN!**

Then Shrimpy did something **AMAZING**.
He took a deep breath and for the first
time ever he didn't worry or feel scared.
He actually began to play.
And do you know what?

He had **FUN!** His friends all cheered.
"You're **NOT** wimpy! Hooray for Shrimpy!"

Yippee!